For the Unborn

For the Unborn

Books by Steven F. White

POETRY

Burning the Old Year (Unicorn, 1984)
For the Unborn (Unicorn, 1986)

PROSE

Culture and Politics in Nicaragua (Lumen Books, 1986)

TRANSLATIONS

Poets of Nicaragua 1916-1979 (Unicorn, 1982)
Poets of Chile 1965-1985 (Unicorn, 1986)

STEVEN F. WHITE

For
the
Unborn

1986

Greensboro, North Carolina
Unicorn Press, Inc.

Grateful acknowledgement is made to the editors and publishers of the following periodicals where some of these poems appeared:

Bloomsbury Review, Latin American Perspectives, Northwest Magazine (Portland Oregonian).

The image *Hydra* on the cover is copyright © 1986 by the artist, Arthur Secunda. *All rights reserved.*

Library of Congress Cataloging in Publication Data
White, Steven F., 1955-
  For the unborn.
  I. Title
PS3573.H47478B8   1986   811.'54   86-11111
ISBN 0-87775-193-5
ISBN 0-87775-194-3 (pbk.)

The publisher gratefully acknowledges support from The National Endowment for the Arts, a Federal Agency, and the North Carolina Arts Council, a State Agency, during the time this book was prepared.

For the Unborn was typeset by Anita Richardson in *Baskerville* type; printed by Inter-Collegiate Press on *Plainwell Natural Neutral,* an acid-free sheet; and casebound by Sarah Lindsay in Holliston Mills' *Sail Cloth.* Teo Savory and Alan Brilliant edited and designed this book, published by:

Unicorn Press, Inc.
Post Office Box 3307
Greensboro, NC 27402

FOR NANCY

Who knows the
power of words.

Arthur Secunda
10·12·86
L.A.

TABLE OF CONTENTS

I

POWER AND REBELLION

Opening Fire

the wind   I breathe   then my voice
recites page after page of sky   these poems
naming the storms of history   but not one place
not one time   because even as I write   Chile
disintegrates   falls between my fingers
like the sand of its coast and desert   I say
Santiago   and it melts like the cordillera's snow
I see the year I lived there   decompose   and blow
beyond my face   then I feel my self   lose its form
and the energy that binds me   becomes   the abundance
of light in all our faces   lifetimes of blood
because we are   we will be   here
stronger than the circle of burning   words to come

The Black Bridge

Over land that lights
itself with fear and waters
emptying into
fever, a bridge
arches from decade to
decade longer than anyone
has been alive. This is
the road above reason
where men in uniforms
with briefcases
chained to their wrists
walk to work through
time buying
and selling our silence.

Hard days
for us: that sense of air
beneath our feet, the shadow
of steel spanning our lives.
The planet traveled
so far to have its throat
slit by our atoms. Yet

we have the tremendous
faith of those who believe in
nothing. The eyes
of vengeance
are impenetrably
clear like the hours
that remain. We've seen
how truth was extracted
from us like any metal
and how suffering receives
history with the patience
of a sick child linked
to death by a cough.

We've seen the secret face sculpted
by the pain of victories
and defeats in which we played
no part. We've seen how someone
dies so as not
to change. Is there no

other choice
except to let
generals go
from beginning
to beginning without
end until the
bridge where they
pass through a dream
of power
falls
with the atmosphere?

Some of us
have climbed the bridge
to jump
into nothingness.
But others work
below the enemy
to live history's
seismic changes.

Nations float
on the fire
beneath them—
and within us.

The Debt

We used to gather before dawn
to descend into the enormous throat.
The veins we extracted were our own.
Days became the indelible
nights of our lungs.
And we breathed
at a hundred hours per second.

A hand tightened around our throats.
Someone wanted us to live
on the verge of death
for as long as possible.

We went hungry.
We sold everything,
even our blood.
But it was never enough
when they changed their numbers.

What we owed
finally walked toward them
across our poisoned land
through clouds of dust.
With each step more trees fell
and jungles shrank
to the size of an enemy's head.

But what were they thinking
all those years before they crashed
in their towers of glass—
that they would never be held responsible?

Rage

They burst into the minds
of the living to look
for us. They made a
road of our bodies
which they had opened
to implant
the larvae of fear.

Hide the typewriter!
The police are searching
the house next door!

Single file, herded
toward iron questions
while their blows
rained down.

Yes, they occupied
the hollows of our lives—
until we rose
to become the sky
filling with the storm
we are.

Offering

Our essence burns
and clouds the sky
above the cemetery
where we were uprooted
as we grew from the dead.

The children at school watch the smoke
and pay no attention to their teacher.
Tonight they will dream of gunfire
and the mutilated bodies
of mother or father among the weeds.

Prisoner of Conscience

She heard a fly buzz when she died,
the blue fly that hovers,
hovers around the future corpse
and waits to lay its eggs.

She heard a fly buzz when she died.
The fly with golden wings
and burning eyes announcing death
proceeds across her hand.

She heard a fly buzz, then she died
in her cell with the fly.
No one knows if it eats or drinks.
No one knows, no one knows.

This House

You better get the hell out of here! Don't you know where you are? This is the north side of the river. The only people who come over here are in coffins on their way to the General Cemetery. I know what I'm talking about. I've lived here all my life. People take one look at you and they know you're not from around here. Keep walking. See this house? Don't even look at it. It was first built as a place for the plague victims, but that was seventy years ago when I was a kid. When the sick people died, they were carried like produce through the open market in carts drawn by men. Later, scientists studied bacteria here and kept cages of rabid dogs for their experiments. Then, some years later, when the School of Medicine over on Independencia burned down, laboratories were brought to this house so future doctors could dissect rats in the basement. After the military coup, the torturers moved in and filled the cages with human beings. They brought doctors with them to keep the prisoners alive for questioning. These doctors are experts. They can make pain even more excruciating. They say it is for the good of the country. Everyone knows about this house. Didn't you read the newspapers last week? I live in this neighborhood and I saw what happened from my window. A man stopped right where we are now, doused himself with gasoline, and shouted, *Death must no longer be hidden!* Then he set himself on fire. His two children were tortured here—vivisected in this house.

Secret Police

The screams of the tortured.
That crackling is the invisible traveler's
body of electricity
hallucinating through the ages or seconds,
blindfolded,
descending steps into fire
and the memory of pain.

These are nights of more threats than stars.
I hear my breathing
with its sense of order
on the other side of the door.
We have been divided by fear
into separate lives.

The secret police move through us
as if we were riverbeds,
the fangs of a snake,
chimneys, stems,
the barrel of a gun,
the aorta that carries our dreams.
But in the end, the loss of blood
is always ours.

Over deserted streets,
smoke spirals from burning tires
like the thoughts no body can contain
when the door crashes open at night.
Tomorrow when we disappeared
we belong to nothing,
faces abandoned in archives.

What identity remains
for the anonymous?

Power

If the people lose their fear of power
there will appear, then, a power
as great as the fear that grows in those in power.

The time will come when we fight like water:
river deepening the gorge
or overflowing its banks.

Rebellion

At night the snow creeps slowly
down the mountains in the east.
An entire family with just bread
and tea for weeks.
It's easier to stay in bed
and try to sleep forever.

Rain on metal roofs
and candles flickering
through walls of wood.
The smell of smoke
as a woman stands fanning
some hissing coals.

The laughter of boys
who stagger into shadows
with a can of glue.
And there's the girl without her toys
who waits in a drop of light
on the same corner every night.

No one knows where Iván lives,
but he's on time to all the meetings.
He's too young and knows nothing
but what he's fighting.
He'll wake up tomorrow
and proceed according to plan.

So, there you have it—
nothing.
No food. No work.
Iván is looking
for fire, blood and anything
he can break.

A Natural Turn of Events

Spring in the city and death
has come to our windows.
Behind weapons are eyes that close
so many lives. The poor are cut down
at random in their homes by soldiers
or pulled naked into the night
and placed in the flames of barricades.
Why are we to lament, then,
the general riddled by light this morning?
In the high interests of peace?
The peace that fades in the trees
like the laughter of a lost generation?
Someone needs this blood to glue
one day to the next.
Let the violent dawns
be embedded in all these bodies
to keep them cold,
to keep them dying
into more anniversaries
so we can divide time
into perennial crimes.
What else is there? Tell me.
But use different words—
ones that aren't buried in mass graves,
ones that aren't tangled with the skeletons
who taught this regime how to speak.
Citizens are being turned inside out!
Assassins bolt from cloud to cloud!
Hail destroys the blossoms!
There is talk of dialogue, transition,
the rebirth of democracy.
We've forgotten:
violence is the midwife of history.
I'll bet my life on it.

To Be Human Is to Bury

Let us gather the faces of the fallen,
these leaves of a moving forest,
this debris of an occupied city.
What is it? It's hard to say.
Our days could have been strawberries
floating in a pitcher of red wine
or friends lifting full glasses
around a wooden table in the sun.

But the years of brutality, piercing us
at the speed of light,
are the way they are
as if they always were
and we hate without knowing why.
The radio says that dissidents
will be exterminated like rats.
Life hardens as if it were a piece of bread.

Whoever plants winds, harvests storms—
that's how the saying goes. There was
never really any doubt: to be
human is to bury. Yet even as thousands
of us mourn our dead
and cover the graves we opened,
the Special Forces beat us
inside the cemetery walls.

Alliances

Open in the air of despair!
Thrive from the alliance
of earth and water we are!
Live for us today
even if your offspring are shadows
who will never learn resistance!

We listen as you bend
in wind, alone,
stranger at the crossing
of our times.
Open, open,
open!

Did You Hear the Story?

We have a cocaine house
on Cocaine Hill.
We have a cocaine dog
and a cocaine cat.
We even have a cocaine rat.
We water the plants
with cocaine blood
and fly the leaves out
in cocaine planes
that land in the jungle
on portable strips.
We got the generals in our pockets
and the politicians, too.
When democracy gets bad for business
we pay cocaine money for a cocaine coup.
We have well-armed troops
to protect the crops.
We're doing our part
to make more jobs.
The people up north
living their cocaine days
don't know shit
about the cocaine trade.
'Cause we're dancing on the corpses,
putting their heads on stakes.
And we'll do what's good for business
until it snows over the Amazon!

Stumbling Home Past Curfew in Santiago, Chile

The miracle of wine
multiplying
on my birthday.
There were only three
of us to witness
our table populated
with green bottles,
all as empty as the bar.
Samuel made a final
toast to his foreign
friend's anniversary.
Salud!

From diminishing
smoke, a waitress shouted,
"Hey, have you guys forgotten
about the curfew?" She was
sweeping cigarette butts
from the stained wooden floor
while the bartender snored.
Had we? Had we crossed
that line? Were we situated
on a plane governed
by some supreme, irrational
system of logic?

What time
was it, anyway?
I needed a new wristwatch.
The strict hands
had stopped
on their shining,
circular path
and I hoped
that some part of me
remained
in the safety of those lost
hours before curfew.

Soon I was stumbling
home alone
on the back streets,
past curfew and past
a winter solstice
in my coldest June,
counting my years
to myself, and wishing
I had learned
to count stars
before fingers
as a child.

A block away, someone
coughed. A soldier
stepped from darkness
with a rifle. He didn't
see me. For a second,
I almost believed the wine
had made me invisible
and that I was
already asleep at home,
dreaming with all my blood,
my open capillaries
and my hummingbird heart!

From the Mouths of Babes

A soldier severs a child's tongue
and life parades between decrees.
The nights are thorns in my sleeping face.
A water cannon blasts bees
from the monuments where we swarmed. And the fury
of dogs and clubs surging from clouds that burn!

We suffer at the hands of others.
But their fault is my own disharmony at work.
If I could love, I would see the nowhere but now
with its torches and a road that never ends.
It is not for nothing the way is lit
by the eyes of the oppressed.

II

FOR THE UNBORN

I

This history is for the unborn
who will never enter life,
not for the living who will die
in a cloudburst of light blossoming over cities
on a day we must already remember.
And in the absence that cannot be imagined,
death shall have no dominion
because death will have swallowed itself whole.

On a string I have life,
on a string I have death.
Who am I?
You are the candle
we lit so we could see.

You make me singing,
you buy me crying
and you use me without seeing.
Who am I?
You are the coffin,
the empty one. Because this death
will be different. No one to make you,
buy you, no one to use you.
No one.

I live in a place
guarded by ivory soldiers.
I'm the red snake,
the king of lies.
Who am I?
You are the tongue.
And we believed you.

Before you pass from death to life,
before the first sounds
cross your salty lips struck by light,
before your faces turn in shifting skies
and arms then legs push free

to dry in the smell of the wind,
imagine the planet
consumed by a blaze
that we will give you with your blood.

II

I wrapped myself in a sheet
and made my way to the point
where the two rocks offshore
formed a passage to another world.
He heard my call that night.
I remember the creaking of oars,
the luminous wake above the waves,
the splinters of the battered gunwales,
the back of a man who swung the oars
inside the boat, wiped his forehead
with a sleeve and turned to greet me.
But I wasn't dead. I was alive and young
and laughed on the cliffs of what I knew.

What the gull observes
as it drops toward the sea
changes from an insect with only two legs
moving slowly back and forth across the water
to a rowboat and a man
who watches the last light of the day
lift shadows from a receding shore.
A dolphin leaps from wave to wave.
The wind is from the north.
A storm closes the horizon.

There he is on the point again.
Today the healer mourned his death
and swept his soul right out the window with a broom.
He slipped through bars of sunlight
and left with the dust in his room.
But this time he can scream at me and these waters
from the two rocks that are his mother's knees
until the end of the world that invented us.
I'll never ferry him anywhere.

III

Father, why did the waters rise and flood the land?
The serpent of the sea lifted the waves and sang
with the rain that battered our shores.
What happened then?
The serpent of the land that loves us
made mountains and the people climbed
and the waters rose and from the peaks
we saw our dead floating among the trunks of trees.
Father, do you think it will rain
now as long as it did then?
No. But while we wait for the skies to clear
we can mend sails, repair nets and paint the boat.

All the cities on earth were waiting
for the storm that was not a storm to begin.
The metaphysical one,
the unnatural one.
And the people did nothing.
No one did anything except those who piled weapons
until they reached the clouds. And the people
built their lives on these mountains.

I was one of them.
Like an island, I dressed myself in distance
ready to let centuries slip like dust
between my fingers, ready to let generations
become the chain of fissioned nuclei
that would silence the dead for the first time
and link me to nothingness. An unreal
firestorm whipping an imaginary coast
where I hide in a nonexistent bay
that protects my formless boat.
The invisible rain falling through my eyes
as well as those of the unborn waiting at their window.
The current running colder in me
toward something not within
the stream of human time
had given me a body numb to the world.

The smell of oblivion is in my hair.
The roar of a sea that is not a sea is in my ears.
So this is the journey to the end of the world.

IV

It was up to us to invent the New World,
and with stories of gold
we got the money to do it.
I didn't care under what flag I sailed.
The ships embarked
to distribute our imaginations
throughout the blank maps of our time.
But what could we promise the crews?
Riches? At first it would work.
Their lives? I remember
how my men stared into darkness for years
then turned their eyes on me.
The fear of not being was enough
to kill their Captain.
And I'm surprised they didn't.
After the putrid water ran out
and we boiled the last rice in seawater.
After we ate rats, leather and sawdust mixed with worms.
After storms that snapped masts and shredded sails.
After I killed the mutineers and had their bodies quartered.
After the crew got sick and we tossed the dead
overboard corpse by corpse.
After one of the ships deserted and sailed for home.
But there was that fire on the far shore of intuition
suddenly appearing in a passage to another world.
We brought the water to these sealess coasts.
We put each rock and finger of earth in place
and then we gave them names.
Let these lands burn in the minds of the dreamers.

Peace. Let the water hold these stars.
Under violet skies, the kind that betray,
children from villages adrift in a labyrinth of islands
wave to the wake of a ship passing in their ancestors' dreams.
The sails billow in the same wind
of time lived and unlived
that fills tomorrow's lungs.

The night is mirrored ahead of her ship
as if she were navigating the sky
in the channels of those children's hands.
She is the survivor who drowned in memory,
the only witness to what cannot be remembered.
Those who created her would drift
toward her music and lights
and drop anchor in the eyes of the other world
so she could go on living in their dreams,
so she could give them the power to change what they saw
into the trunk of a cypress covered with crows
floating deeper into the fog.
The fear of not being would have been enough
to save them if it had existed.
But she's what's impossible,
the lie below the sun at night,
the one who sails with the fire
that leaves a desert in its wake
and finally freezes the planet.

V

Ice thundering from towers of ice.
A single eye anchored in the thunder
of centuries of dreams, shipwrecks
and wars that all led to this.
Children of fire, rest here.
What you could have been is over.
Rest with your weapons frozen in ice.
Rest with your armies in the cold fire.
Listen to their limbs snap in night after night of silence.
Towers of ice toppling into a bottomless lake
and another chunk of history sends waves
to shatter on the far shore.
These jagged arches resemble the cities you destroyed
but they are not the ruins of civilizations,
only the absence of humanity.
To climb these heights of ice
means not to be born,
means finding no stone
shaped by human hands.

This river of ice carrying what was once alive.
This river of ice growing and receding in time
as if it were alive in the blue fissures of extinction.
This river of ice scarring a granite face.
Children of fire, rest here.

Strange to see pieces of ice
unexpectedly accost the boat
in water that turned grayer
than the time it takes to age.
Egrets rising from swamps
on either side of the narrow channel.
Who named these places
Leopard's Tongue and Gulf of Elephants?
Then entering the lake in a blast of wind.
Then watching the Indians drop their oars
and scramble for the cold ashes
they had brought
to make their faces black,
to stay alive
when the glacier appeared
shining in the distance.

Peel back the eyelids of earth
and you will see the solemn procession
of icebergs sailing with the wind
that slashes the eyes of the dead.
At the heart of each iceberg
is the flame that steers it
into the greater death
beyond the ruptured membrane of the cell
where we all could have lived in peace.

VI

If these charred and frozen words
were the unborn's dream of never being
that found its way into the language of the living,
if hope in its interval of space and time
were to flash its warning as a guide,

let us tell the heads of state
that the borders of their countries
have been erased and that there is nothing
left to defend but life itself.

We're the four brothers and sisters
who live all over the world:
one runs but never gets tired,
another whistles but has no mouth,
another drinks but could always drink more,
another eats but it's never enough.
Who are we?
You are the water we drink,
the air we breathe, the land we work
and the fire we use to cook and keep warm.

Everyone asks about me
but I don't ask about anyone.
Everyone walks on me,
but I don't walk on anyone.
Who am I?
You are the road,
the one we decided to take.

A forest
of trees with twelve branches,
on each branch four nests,
and in each nest seven birds.
Who are we?
You are the years,
months, weeks and days
that we want to go on living.

A thermal pulse is my pulse.
I know what it would mean.
I remember every missile
planted in my body before I was born.
I remember when my enemies vanished.
I remember how everything that dies
is simply an exchange for what comes alive.

III

CROSSING THE PLAIN OF PATIENCE

Songs for the Beginnings

1

Someone awakens inside us.
The walls of our bodies dissolve.
We uproot the gods
whose only names were numbers
in the network of gods
we implanted in silos
below fields of wheat.
We rip them
from our dying lips,
break them
into the most basic words
so we can learn to speak again.

2

Rain shocks our tongues with its purity
and returns to the sky with our song.
Clouds keep emptying into a three-shored river
that flows both ways and is still
at the same time,
that rises and unfurls in space
like a great ribbon of light.
As we drink from this river
before we are born,
we forget enough to enter life.
Then finally the waters
disappear in our memory of death.

3

So much traveling
away from ourselves.
It's impossible to return.
But we do,
even though what we were
no longer exists.
Our dreams manipulated us
as we rose with them
then fell back
to earth
just to kill each other
over and over.

4

Someday like mountains
emerging from the water
to occupy a form
that already existed in the air,
we'll lift stones on our backs—
one for each injustice we've committed.
Higher and higher into the heart of the sky
until we reach the snowstar.
And from that height within us
we'll see ourselves
flowing into another life
distant, but still ours.

5

Father mountain, don't be angry.
We arrived on the tomorrow that has been
and the yesterday that will be.
The boulders that once were
wedged between your ribs
followed our song to the peak.
When we descend,
broken and changed
under our burden of ice,
forgive us and let there be no rage.
Father snow, don't hurt us on the paths.
Let us go safely to the Lake of All Ends.

6

That star will give us its light!
The one shining like an orphan of snow
between peaks of darkness that found us
in this strange village
in a house that isn't ours.
Is the river our mother because we're alone?
Is the stone our father because we're poor?
Will clouds be our mother and wind our father?
Our parents are everything that happens.
A black storm gallops in the sky.
If there is no rock to hear us,
in what night can we wander lost?

7

Your chest is that rock.
Your eyes, that night.
There was only one of you who didn't return
from the beginnings with a song.
I found him alone on the summit
beside one pile of stone and another of ice.
In the storm and the hail,
in the deep snow below glaciers,
he was trying to bury himself.
He spoke of someone who used to cry
with him in the wind and the cold,
someone he could not find.

The Shadow

> *"El Huascarán nos miraba*
> *y entonces fue que sentimos*
> *su blancura imperdonable."*
>
> Rodolfo Hinostroza

My father was buried alive over there, sir,
near the four dead palm trees
where the center of Yungay used to be.
Now there's nothing—just tourists like you
taking photographs of the white crosses
scattered below us. 20,000 dead.
No one believes me when I say it.
Less than fifty survivors. And most of them children.

Because we were all at the circus!
That day the bright tents rose at the end
of the road used only by weeping families in black.
The tremors began and stopped. We waited.
Then we heard the thunder that went on and on.
My mother ran with me in her arms, tripped,
screamed at me: "Go to the cemetery!"
It's the only high place in the valley.

Days passed and we were stranded
among the old ghosts overlooking the sea
of mud and debris, the vast fresh grave
of the world as we knew it. The whole time,
I looked up at the mountain that had betrayed us.
Its eyes would rumble open
sending avalanches of snow
down a face that would never be the same.

I am the shadow of that disfigured head.
And I'll be here if you ever return.

The Elders

From the delta, from days blank with snow
lifted in circles from the surface of their faces,
from the substance of being,
from villages lost along the way of the white clouds,
    they come with signs of the creator.

Brushed by the raven's wing into another life,
marked by a beak of ice that etches a trail
across their minds, separated from their bodies
stacked like cordwood by the doors of earthen huts,
    they come with signs of the creator.

With masks and songs and incandescent seeds,
with holes in their spirit hands so as not to grasp
all life, with the animals that escaped and multiplied,
with a heavy load of skins and sinews, bones and feathers,
    they come with signs of the creator.

I see them following a line of driftwood along the shore,
getting closer to where I wait beneath my eyelids.
They are wearing wooden goggles with thin slits.
They pierce the lips of silence with their labrets
    as they come with signs of the creator.

On great sleds they glide across equations
based on principles of violence that destroyed the living.
I hear the wind's invisible dogs. Soon the elders will chant
their cycles of fulfillment and I will join them
    for they have come with signs of the creator.

Once We Carved Steps

Once we carved steps into the tree of the world
and climbed to where our god is no less than the sky.
Once we painted seasons and suns on drums with blood.
There were children to inherit our language.

But we could not survive ourselves.
Each death could have joined us
but we drifted farther apart,
galaxies expanding, light years between words.

Beasts made of stars drink from the white
river of our silence.

Rituals

Here are the trails of dust and blood
where the faithful crawled for kilometers in the sun
to the virgin tyrant deep within themselves.
They wept at what they saw.
Here are the banks of candles, the bright costumes,
the church, the songs, and waves of pilgrims.

We finally leave the horned demons behind
as they dance from bonfires
and gore the midnight sky again
and again, as years become frenzied centuries.
We leave the plaza throbbing
with drums and dreams and bells.

We walk into the desert
that surrounds the village
and look for a place to sleep in the sand.
In the distance we still hear all their hearts
beating the rhythm WE ARE, WE ARE ONE
in the continuum of ritual.

The fog covers the stars
and envelops us like some other
form of consciousness.
Our thoughts roll beyond our borders.
Anything can happen now.
Your hand slips from mine.

I'm frightened!
So far from any miracle.
And I believe
in nothing.

Crossing the Plain of Patience

The return from our past was always painful.
Because it wasn't as if we had regained life,
but that we had lost it once again
in the earth covered with what grows.
We found ourselves
thinking of the barren place,
remembering how we would cross
the plain of patience
and navigate dunes in fierce winds
below a sun that watched us like an open wound.

Here was the paradise we could seek forever.
Only our particles dispersed like light.
Only the alternate deserts of our lives.
Only the absence of desire.

Where we left our dreams
and flooded our fields
and measured each syllable of water,
was the edge of the oasis.
Then we would step into desolation
and a stronger vision:
the night so clear
we could hear the stars
and the dead who had slept like babies
in their womb of sand
as they soared over the great necropolis.

The desert rocks were our eyes—
bare, beyond moisture, ductless.
It made no sense to weep
for trees that never were.

There was no longing for the life
that shriveled and blew through immensity
or for all the lives that disappeared
in the void of history.

For the desert was the emptiness that grew
within us and, here, our prayers
rose without fear from a handful of dust.
Everything we could have known
knelt before us
as if we were greater than what we knew.

The Hands of God

The force that joins single
acts of trying to turn
a good profit
is the unseen
hand of God,
according to Apostle Adam
Smith. And it makes
sense in a God
eat God world.

A drunk poet
from a banana
republic warned
that something apocalyptic
would pour from the invisible
hand. But who knows?

I can speak only for
myself.
Baptized in the impure
waters that wrinkle
this plain, I was
given a name
to remind me
of the times that eat
their own children.

When I lose hope and fear
is the only thing that keeps
me going, I try
not to think
of you as you look
for me day and
night in your freezing palm,
as you toss handfuls
of whiteness
over all the dead years.

The White Train

The white train carries images
of ourselves, segments
time with its linked
cars like verbs
of all tenses,
and passes through our brains
as an impulse that erases
the future and our forward
dreaming. Its final
destination is the nucleus
of the open sky or the open
sky of the nucleus.

The white train is a backbone,
curving through the space
we inhabit—our neighborhoods
and nightmares. To move
from car to car among the vertebrae
is to enter the central
consciousness.

The white train transports
more than warheads
and classified material conceived
in sterile institutions.
I've seen the car
where brides in long white dresses
walk just above the fields of blinding snow.
I've seen the car
where a saint transcribes the vision
of clothing washed white in blood,
of a pale horse galloping from fog.
I've seen the car
where the empty pages of an immense book
flutter in the wind
like banners of surrender.
I've seen the car
where the white flukes of a whale
disappear under waves littered with debris.

I've seen the car
with stacks of ivory beside stacks
of non-white bodies
and bags of human ears
held by smiling colonizers.
I've seen the car
where figures in white hoods and robes
encircle a burning cross.

There is car after car filled
with the bones and skulls of those
who loved and moaned between sheets
stained with semen. Moonlight
illuminates the remains
of what we were so desperate to smuggle
across life's borders
in the all-night train.

Some official has decided
to paint the train's whiteness
the colors of the earth.
Only the top will be white
to reflect sunlight. Now, perhaps children
will put pennies on the tracks
leading to the nothing that is
and perhaps the white
train will seem identical to all the other trains
passing through the stations of the seasons.

We are passengers of the white train
even when we watch it pass in silence.
We are passengers
even when we form human barricades
and carry signs that say:
"Stop the white train's cargo of death!"
There is no way to say goodbye
to the train that runs along an optic nerve
through blurred landscapes
bearing the weight of darkness.

Abandoned at 4,000 Meters

A sudden jolt and everything stops.
We're on the border
of madness. All the zeros
on this money from Bolivia
make me nervous,
make my backpack heavier.

It is night but no one sleeps
on our decapitated train
dead on the tracks
of a single desert
divided into two countries.

I see the engine
chug toward the stars
leaving its body behind.

And my poor pounding head!

Workers in dirty overalls
come from nowhere
with tools
and too much time.
They begin to crawl beneath us.

Speculators wonder if their bones
will be checked for contraband.
They would even invest in this darkness
for the tiniest of profits.

I shiver by a window
that is useless because here
the wind blows through glass.

The Clouds

Today, the clouds
from a place that had slipped my mind
caught up with me and demanded satisfaction.
I admit it wasn't fair for me to forget them—
the way they spilled
over the volcano's rim
where I once stood,
drifted down to cover the great eye
of a lake far below,
rebounded in slow motion,
rising,
then gradually filled the crater
in the most incredible silence.
The truth is, I didn't know
what to make of them then.
But they're here now and it's clear
that they have discovered
the power of returning and leaving.
If I deny them, there's no telling
what might happen after I fall asleep
and the clouds are free
to cross the boundaries of dream.
I realize they may come back at any time,
years from now, and claim to be
everything I will ever think,
or the life I squandered with words,
or someone I love,
or the heart of wars and ambitions.
They may stay and hide the edge
of the void where I need to stand.
Or perhaps they'll whisper some advice
just before I die to become the perfect
traveler outside all language.
A song comes from the fog around me
in a tongue I don't understand.
I hear small bells.
A barefoot woman dressed in rags
passes with her flock of sheep.
What are the clouds trying to say?
Now I remember.

Time

This is the perfect place to taste
the sea inside you and I kneel
between your legs with an intolerable
thirst for the future. Then you
straddle both my coasts
and reach back
through warm summer wind,
through the night of our species,
through time like a mantra,
to caress my thighs. Soon your lips
part, eyes close, and so much breath
escapes. A drop of sweat
rolls between your breasts.

Somewhere a wave
of light over our contours
breaks. The point of contact
between seasons
might be skin on skin or
your legs wrapped
around mine or not knowing
where my body ends
and yours begins. Or is it
the instant that closes
upon itself to enter
a time of no human
awareness at all?

As we roll apart and sigh
then kiss, a skeletal
prehistoric fish lays
luminous eggs across the sky.

No Name

If the final heartbeat were enough
to propel my blood farther
from its center than it had
ever gone, beyond strictures
of skin, then I would
send with it a message
to my disciples
asking them to return.

They set out with my thoughts—
or were they my thoughts themselves?
Even if my blood overtakes them,
they may not recognize this liquid
that smells of sunrise, in which they
could plunge and
discover all the lost
connections of their days.

My blood would follow the curving
earth, reach the forest shaken
by wind, the air filled with yellow
leaves, the rain falling
on my closed eyelids
where forever has gone
to seed before
ever taking root.

There, I'll remember my disciples
gathering in the exact place
where the losing and finding
of the self occurs—they
who abandoned me, who speak
with wisdom, who journey
to convince the world
I never lived.

One by One

So calm now—
and the questions,
one by one,
come down to a stream.

Are the steppingstones
in the current
our scattered limbs
from another time
when we knew ourselves
as whole as the world?

And in the canyon's
long blue pools
how can we distinguish ourselves
floating in a body of water
that takes our shapes
only to dissolve them?

We enter that life
between cliffs
that once were lips.
A forgotten language returns.

The Other House

As if human history
were concentrated
in the dream of a single word
and each letter of that word
were a different language
and the word itself
were all the languages on earth.

As if that word
were suddenly easy to abandon
and we could enter the other house
purged of ourselves, transparent,
so healed that our bodies
seemed only a mirage
like the crumbled cities far below.

We remember a voice
speaking of the other house
and how the length and the breadth
and the height of it would be equal.
True, but once inside
we know there are no walls.
Only a source of light nothing can contain.

The Seeds

Neither dead nor alive, like us,
from here we can see them
floating across oceans,
guided by currents and a map of tides.
They carry storms and quiet afternoons
in roots and leaves
compressed to almost nothing.
The seeds know only the country
of sunlight, earth and rain.

And there are the ones carried by men,
measured, bought, sold and stolen by men
who sail time's bleeding forehead.
We've seen the seeds cultivated
in the mountain's shadow, harvested,
moved on water through machines, dried,
moved on water in ships to distant lands,
roasted, ground and brewed in water
that moves down millions of throats.

Others fly in hands of wind,
island to island, mind to mind,
invisible, moving through the auras
of their limits, ready to push life
through openings that do not exist,
carrying a memory of sky to the earth
where seasons circle, transforming
silence into more seeds.

Transportation

I've been floating for the past
several pages
of my life.
Maybe too much for my own good.
Maybe not enough.
I don't know.

I was going to cross
the frozen emptiness between two stars
that is the distance
between my eyes.

But more people got on the bus
with sacks of corn and squawking hens
and babies on their backs
and old women began vomiting behind me
and the bus kept winding higher
into thinner and thinner mountain air.

The wolves of light
were on the verge of teaching me
how to run with them
in a foreign sky
and how they take part of the past
into their lungs with each breath.

But the stench of sweat and urine
and rotten fruit was overwhelming.

I had almost erased myself completely
and was ready to be drawn
out of this world
through a hole between clouds.

But I stood up and gave my seat
to an old woman
bent by a dripping load of animal guts
which she dropped on my foot.
Then she sat down and smiled.
No teeth. I smiled, too.

I was dizzy, sick and lucky
to feel so human.
It's true! And the little guy beside me
was about to pick my pocket!

About the Author

Steven F. White was born in Abington, Pennsylvania in 1955 and was raised in Glencoe, Illinois. He was educated at Williams College and the University of Oregon. His awards include the Academy of American Poets Prize in 1975 and 1977 as well as the Hubbard Hutchinson Fellowship from Williams College which enabled him to travel and to work in various Latin American countries. In 1983, he received a Fulbright grant to translate poetry in Chile. He and his wife are currently living in Eugene, Oregon.

In addition to his first volume of poetry, *Burning the Old Year*, Mr. White has edited and translated two bilingual anthologies of Latin American poetry for Unicorn Press: *Poets of Nicaragua: 1916-1979* and *Poets of Chile: 1965-1985*. He also compiled a book of interviews with Nicaraguan writers entitled *Culture and Politics in Nicaragua* (Lumen Books).